The Goddess of Love

at the Funfair

Ulrich Germania

Imprint

Book title:
The Goddess of Love at the Funfair

Subtitle:
A fair with a mystical flair

Series:
Romantic Encounters at the Funfair

AI Note:
AI generated story, initiated and revised by the author
Translated from German into American English by an AI.

Author:
Ulrich Germania © 2025

Publisher:
BoD · Books on Demand GmbH, In de Tarpen 42,
22848 Norderstedt, bod@bod.de

Print:
Libri Plureos GmbH, Friedensallee 273,
22763 Hamburg

ISBN: 978-3-7693-5575-8

Table of contents

Picture credits:

The images on the book cover and the illustrations in the book were generated by AI and modified using programs for photo manipulation.

AI Note:

Author Ulrich Germania came up with the characters and the plot, the AI wrote the story, then it was revised and improved. The translation from German into American English was also done by an AI. It was checked and approved.

Encounter at the Funfair

It was a balmy summer evening when the two friends Mia and Suzy strolled through the funfair in high spirits. The colorful lights and cheerful music magically attracted them, and they enjoyed the exuberant atmosphere. Mia, with her long blonde hair and bright blue eyes, and Suzy, with her dark curls and infectious laugh, were real eye-catchers.

They laughed and chatted as they walked past the various stands, snacked on candy floss and marveled at the rides. Just as they were thinking about which ride they wanted to try next, they were approached by two young men.

"Hey, you two! Would you like to go for a ride on the Ferris wheel with us?" asked one of them, a tall, sporty guy with a charming smile. His friend, a little smaller but with a mischievous grin, nodded in agreement.

Mia and Suzy exchanged a quick glance and smiled. "Why not?" Mia replied cheerfully. "We love the Ferris wheel!"

Together they made their way to the Ferris wheel and the two young men introduced themselves. The taller one was called Luke, and his friend was Max.

There were lots of people in front of the Ferris wheel who wanted to go on the ride. While they waited in line, they introduced themselves to each other and it turned out that Luke and Max were very likeable young men, and the girls were delighted to have been approached by these two.

When they finally took their seats in a gondola on the Ferris wheel, they enjoyed the breathtaking view over the funfair and the city. The lights twinkled like stars and the cheerful music filled the air. Mia and Suzy felt like they were in a fairy tale, and the company of Luke and Max made the evening even more special.

They laughed a lot during the trip and got to know each other even better.

When the Ferris wheel came to the final halt, they decided to continue enjoying the evening together and try out even more rides.

After leaving the Ferris wheel, the four young people decided to visit another ride. They strolled through the funfair and let themselves be guided by the colorful lights and cheerful music.

In the end, they opted for the roller coaster, which enticed them with its rapid curves and thrilling descents.

Mia and Max sat down in one carriage, while Suzy and Luke took a seat in the next. The excitement and anticipation were palpable as the rollercoaster slowly climbed up the first hill. Mia and Max held on to the safety bars and exchanged excited glances. Suzy and Luke laughed and joked as they enjoyed the view.

When the roller coaster reached the top of the hill, the world held its breath for a moment.

Then it plunged into the depths, and the four young people screamed with joy and excitement. The rapid curves and loops made their hearts beat faster and they enjoyed every second of the ride.

After the wild rollercoaster ride, they got out of the cars still laughing about the exciting experience.

Mia and Max exchanged conspiratorial glances, while Suzy and Luke also got closer. It was obvious that a special bond was developing between the two couples.

Together, they decided to continue enjoying the evening and try out even more rides. The funfair offered countless opportunities for fun and adventure, and a chance to have fun together and get to know each other better.

As they went from one attraction to the next, they felt their friendships grow stronger and stronger.

As they continued to stroll through the fair, Max took Mia's hand, and she allowed him to do so. A warm feeling flowed through her and she smiled at him.

Suzy noticed her friend Mia walking hand in hand with Max and a smile flitted across her face. She saw how happy Mia looked and she also felt enchanted by the romantic atmosphere of the fair.

Suzy glanced at Luke, who was walking next to her. He seemed a little shy and didn't dare to take her hand. With a determined smile, Suzy reached for his hand and intertwined her fingers with his. Luke was surprised, but then he smiled and squeezed her hand gently.

The four young people walked hand in hand through the fair, enjoying the cheerful music and the colorful lights.

They felt like they were in a fairy tale, and the magic of the evening made their hearts beat faster.

The Witch's Cottage

In keeping with the magical atmosphere, they happened to discover a wooden house on the fairground that looked like a witch's house in a fairytale. The house was made of dark wood and decorated with ornate carvings. The windows were small and round, with colorful stained glass that sparkled in the light of the fair. A narrow chimney protruded from the roof, from which a thin thread of smoke rose and was lost in the balmy summer air.

An old woman who looked like a witch was sitting in front of the little house. Her face was deeply wrinkled and her eyes sparkled mysteriously. She wore a long, black dress that reached the ground and a pointed hat that sat crookedly on her head. Her hands were bony and marked with age spots, and she held a gnarled walking stick that looked as if it had been carved from an ancient tree.

A black bird sat on her shoulder, watching the four young people with its sharp eyes. But it wasn't a raven, rather an owl. A black cat rested on her lap, stretching lazily and purring softly.

The old woman smiled mysteriously when she saw the group approaching, and her presence lent the scene a magical yet eerie atmosphere.

"Welcome, my dears," said the old woman in a croaky voice. "Come closer and let me tell you something."

Mia, Suzy, Max and Luke exchanged curious glances and stepped closer to the witch's house. The old woman stroked the black cat on her lap and the bird on her shoulder cawed softly.

"I can see that you are looking for something special," the old woman continued. "Perhaps I can help you fulfill your wishes. But be warned, sometimes things are not what they seem."

The four young people were fascinated and a little nervous.

"What do you mean?" Mia asked cautiously.

The old woman smiled mysteriously.

"Each of you has a desire in your heart that you may not even want to admit to yourself. I can help you to recognize these wishes and perhaps even fulfil them. But to do so, you have to trust me and fulfill a small task for me."

Suzy looked at the old woman skeptically.

"And what kind of job would that be?"

The old woman raised a bony hand and pointed to a small, enchanted garden behind the witch's house.

"There are many different flowers in this garden, four of which are special flowers that are meant for you. Each of your flowers represents a wish. Pick a flower and bring it to me and I will tell you more about your wishes."

Mia, Suzy, Max and Luke looked at each other and finally nodded. They were curious and wanted to find out what the old woman had to tell them.

Together they entered the enchanted garden and began to search for the special flowers.

The garden was full of strange plants and bright flowers that shimmered in the moonlight.

Mia asked: "There are so many different beautiful flowers here, how am I supposed to recognize which flower is a special one?"

Luke seemed to sense it: "The flowers are all of equal value. Only when you choose one does it become your own special flower."

It didn't take long for each of them to find a special flower.

Mia picked a bright red flower, Suzy a delicate blue one, Max a bright yellow one and Luke a deep purple one.

They returned to the old woman with the flowers in their hands.

"Very good," she said and took the flowers. "Now let's see what wishes you have in your hearts."

The old woman looked carefully at the flowers and said:

"Each of these flowers represents a wish that you carry in your hearts," she said with a mysterious smile. "Let's see what wishes you have."

She held up the bright red flower that Mia had picked.

"This red flower stands for passion and love," the old woman explained. "Mia, your heart longs for a deep, passionate connection. You wish to find someone who makes your heart glow and with whom you can share an intense love."

Mia blushed slightly, but she couldn't deny that the old woman's words were exactly what she was feeling.

"How do you know my name?" Mia asked the old woman, but the witch didn't answer, just smiled mysteriously.

Everyone in the group was curious to see what the other flowers would reveal.

The old woman took the delicate blue flower that Suzy had picked.

"This flower stands for peace and stability," she said. "Suzy, you want a relationship that gives you security and safety. You are looking for someone who will bring you stability and peace and with whom you can build a harmonious future."

Suzy smiled and felt understood. The old woman's words reflected her deepest wishes.

Next, the old woman held up the bright yellow flower that Max had picked.

"This flower represents joy and adventure," she explained. "Max, you long for a relationship that is full of fun and exciting experiences. You want to find someone who will fill your life with laughter and adventure and with whom you can share unforgettable moments."

Max nodded in agreement and felt encouraged by the old woman's words.

Finally, the old woman took the deep purple flower that Luke had picked.

"This flower represents mystery and depth," she said. "Luke, you want a relationship that is full of mystery and deep emotion. You are looking for someone who touches your soul and with whom you can build a deep and meaningful connection."

Luke felt how the old woman's words touched his heart. He knew that she was expressing exactly what he secretly wished for.

The old woman smiled contentedly. "Now you know the wishes you carry in your hearts," she said. "May the fair help you to fulfill these wishes and find the love you are looking for."

With these words, the old woman said goodbye, went into her witch's house and closed the door behind her.

The four young people stared at the witch's house, lost in thought.

Mia said: "She knew all our names, even though we hadn't introduced ourselves to her."

Max nodded and said: "Very strange indeed. She was like a fortune teller who lets someone draw cards from a deck and then interprets the fate of the chosen cards. She used the flowers instead of playing cards."

Suzy said shakily, "How scary."

Luke said: "And you know what else is scary? She didn't ask us for any money, even though this kind of thing isn't normally offered for free at a funfair."

Max said bravely: "We should talk to her again and offer her some money. I'll go to the witch's house and tell her to come out again."

Mia pleaded: "Don't do it Max, I'm scared for you!"

Max replied: "Calm down, I'll just open the door and call into the cottage for her to come out again."

Max took a few steps towards the witch's house and Luke followed him, while the girls waited at a safe distance from the cottage.

Luke opened the door and Max called out into the emptiness of the dark room: "Hello, can you come out again?", but he received no answer.

"Hello? Where are you? Can you hear me?" Max called out, but again he received no answer. Instead, the black cat came out of the room and the black bird flew out of the door, past Max's head.

The cat climbed onto the wooden house and sat on the roof; the bird flew to the cat and sat next to it.

Max and Luke rejoined Mia and Suzy and together they stared at the bird and the cat, who were sitting confidentially side by side on the roof of the witch's house, looking down at them.

Suddenly the cat sat down on its hindquarters, raised a paw and waved at the two couples as if it were an Asian waving cat.

Max said: "She's waving at us like a Thai lucky cat. I think it's better if we wave back and then move on."

And so they did. All four of them waved goodbye to the cat, then they turned and left the old, mysterious wooden house and plunged back into the noisy hustle and bustle of the fair.

Fulfillment of the Wishes

Max suddenly stopped and looked deep into Mia's eyes.

"Mia, I listened carefully to what the witch said about your wishes. Is what she said true?"

Mia looked at Max and smiled slightly sheepishly.

"Yes, it's true," she replied quietly. "I really want a passionate connection. Someone who makes my heart glow."

Max nodded and took her hand more firmly.

"I think that's beautiful, Mia. I hope I can be that someone for you. I want to get to know you better and find out if we can have that connection."

Mia felt her heart beat faster.

"I'd like to find out too, Max."

Max looked deep into Mia's eyes, his voice full of emotion as he asked:

"May I make your heart glow?"

Mia smiled and felt her heart beat faster.

"Gladly, try it!" she replied quietly, her eyes sparkling with excitement.

Without hesitation, Max grabbed Mia and gently pulled her into his arms. Their bodies were close together and the world around them seemed to stand still for a moment.

Max leaned down and gave her a kiss full of passion. His lips met hers with an intensity that took Mia's breath away.

She suddenly felt a glow in her whole body as she returned Max's passionate kiss. The glow spread to Max and they felt as if they were caught in a magical moment. Their hearts beat for each other and Mia and Max knew that they had found each other.

While they lost themselves in their magical moment, Suzy and Luke watched the action with a smile.

Suzy looked at Luke and sensed that a special bond had formed between them too.

"Luke, what do you think about what the witch said?" she asked quietly.

Luke smiled and took Suzy's hand.

"I think she's right. Yes, I do want a deep and meaningful connection. And I think we could have that connection."

Suzy felt her heart beat faster. "I feel the same, Luke. Let's keep enjoying the evening and see where it takes us."

Luke nodded, pulled Suzy closer to him and gave her a gentle kiss on the forehead. Suzy smiled and felt safe and secure in his company. Together with Mia and Max, they continued their walk through the funfair, hand in hand and full of anticipation for the rest of the evening's experiences.

After a while, they discovered a cozy beer garden with a dance floor. The cheerful music and the laughter of the people attracted them magically. The beer garden was decorated with colorful fairy lights that sparkled in the evening light. The tables and benches were well occupied, and the atmosphere was exuberant and cheerful.

On the dance floor, young and old danced to the live music of a band made up of old men. The musicians wore nostalgic clothing and played the hits of the 60s with great passion. Their instruments were well cared for and the sounds of the guitar, bass, drums and keyboard filled the air. The lead singer of the band was able to adapt his voice very well to the songs and you almost had the feeling that the Rolling Stones or the Beatles were giving a concert on stage.

Mia, Max, Suzy and Luke found a free table near the dance floor and sat down. They ordered drinks and enjoyed the cheerful atmosphere.

The music was infectious, and it wasn't long before they were carried away by the old songs and rock music.

Max stood up and held out his hand to Mia. "Would you like to dance?" he asked with a charming smile.

Mia nodded enthusiastically and took his hand. Together they entered the dance floor and began to move to the beat of the music. Their movements were synchronized and full of joy, and they laughed as they playfully touched and teased each other while dancing.

Suzy watched the two of them and felt infected by the cheerful atmosphere. She turned to Luke and asked: "Would you like to dance too?"

Luke smiled and took her hand. 'I'd love to,' he replied.

Together they joined Mia and Max on the dance floor and danced to the rousing rock music of the live band.

The oldies band on stage played with great dedication and joy, and the old hits were well received by the audience.

The dance floor was full of people moving to the well-known songs. Old and young danced side by side and the boundaries between the generations disappeared.

Mia and Max, as well as Suzy and Luke, were happy. The music, the cheerful atmosphere and not least the fact that everyone had found a partner to love made their hearts beat faster.

The Goddess of Love

When the two couples returned to their table from the dance floor, they noticed that a beautiful blonde woman was sitting there.

Her long, golden hair shone in the light of the fair and her eyes sparkled mysteriously. Max stepped closer and said politely: "Excuse me, this is our table. Can you move a little to the side?"

The beautiful woman moved a little so that everyone had room, smiled kindly and replied: "Yes, I'd love to, I know it's your table. May I introduce myself? I am Amora, a goddess of love and assistant to Cupid, the god of love. I just wanted to make sure that our love arrows didn't miss their target."

Mia, Suzy, Max and Luke looked at each other in surprise. Amora's presence seemed to add to the magical atmosphere of the evening. They sat down at the table and listened intently to what the goddess of love had to tell them.

"I'm glad to see that you've found each other," Amora continued. "The fair is a place full of magic and possibilities, and it seems that fate has brought you together. May your love grow and flourish."

The four young people felt touched by Amora's words but were also very irritated.

Max brought it up: "Beautiful woman, we're here at the fair, there are clowns and charlatans. You saw us together on the dance floor and now you're telling us that you're a goddess of love? Anyone can see that we are two lovers and unfortunately that is no proof that you are a goddess of love. Sorry, I'm irritated.

Amora laughed and asked: "Do you remember your visit to the witch's house and the old woman who made you pick flowers and then revealed your personal, secret wishes?"

Mia, Suzy, Max and Luke looked at each other in surprise and nodded.

"Yes, we do," Suzy replied. "It was a very special moment."

"And suddenly the woman was gone," said Max.

Amora smiled mysteriously.

"Well, I have a confession to make. That old woman was me, in transformed form. I wanted to make sure that your hearts recognize the right wishes and that you have the opportunity to fulfill those wishes."

The four young people were speechless.

"You were the old woman?" Max asked incredulously. "Why did you turn?"

Amora smiled wisely.

"Sometimes it's easier to talk to people not as a beautiful blonde woman, but as an old woman, because then people think they are talking to someone who is wise and experienced. I wanted to help you open your hearts and find the love you are looking for."

Max grabbed his hair and tussled it. "Somehow I still can't believe that you're an old woman and a beautiful goddess of love at the same time. Where are we? At the funfair in real life, or in a fairy tale with witches and gods?"

Amora smiled and raised a hand. "Let me prove to you that I am the goddess of love and that I was the old woman."

At that moment, the black bird that had been sitting on the old woman's shoulder suddenly appeared and landed on the table. It squawked softly and looked at the four young people with its sharp eyes.

Shortly afterwards, the black cat that had been lying on the old woman's lap jumped onto the table and sat down next to the bird. She purred softly and rubbed her head against Amora's hand.

"These two are my faithful companions," Amora explained. "They are always with me, no matter what form I appear in."

Mia, Suzy, Max and Luke looked at the animals in amazement and knew that Amora was telling the truth. The sudden presence of the bird and the cat proved that she was indeed the old woman in transformed form.

"It seems like we really have landed in a fairy tale, doesn't it?" Suzy said quietly and looked Amora questioningly in the eye.

Amora nodded.

"Sometimes the boundaries between reality and fairy tales are blurred. The fair is a place full of magic and possibilities. Use the opportunity you have been given today to fulfill your wishes and find the love you have always been looking for."

After a short pause, during which everyone present was at a loss for words, Amora added;

"I hope that as a goddess of love and an old woman, I was able to help you find the love of your life. Fate is now in your hands, and I will leave you now."

After saying this, Amora slowly rose from her seat.

The black bird spread its wings, flew into the air and sat on Amora's left shoulder, while the black cat gracefully jumped from the table onto Amora's outstretched arm, climbed up and then sat on her right shoulder.

Suddenly, a gentle breeze blew through the beer garden and the fairground lights seemed to shine brighter for a moment.

Amora raised her hands and smiled at the four young people.

"May love always be with you," she said softly.

Then she began to slowly dissolve into a shimmering beam of light. The bird and the cat also disappeared in a soft light that spread around them.

Within moments, Amora and her animals had disappeared as if they had never been there.

The four young people sat there speechless, sensing that they had witnessed a magical moment.

They knew that this evening was very special and that their newfound connections were strong, meaningful and fabulous.

Max looked deep into Mia's eyes and smiled.

"I never thought fairy tales could be true," he said quietly. "But tonight, I learned that there really is magic and the supernatural in life."

Mia returned his smile and squeezed his hand. "Sometimes it just takes the right moment and the right people to discover magic, and today the goddess of love from a fairy tale also helped us," she replied softly.

Luke nodded in agreement and looked at Suzy. "I actually doubted whether true love really exists in life," he confessed, "but now I know that it does and that we've found it."

Suzy smiled and put her hand on his cheek. "True love is often closer than we think. We just have to open our eyes and our hearts to recognize it. Amora has helped us with that."

The four talked for a while about fairy tales and true love, then went back to enjoying the happy atmosphere of the fair and each other's company.

As the fairground lights slowly faded and the night drew to a close, they said goodbye to each other with the promise of seeing each other again soon.

They knew that their story had only just begun and that they would experience many more magical moments together.

More Books by the Author

If you enjoyed this romantic, kitschy story, then you are sure to enjoy other short stories that Ulrich Germania has come up with.

Many stories by the author tell of romantic encounters in unusual places.

AI-Note: For the following stories applies: Ulrich Germania came up with the characters and the plot, the AI wrote the story, and then the author revised and improved it.

Fair of Hearts
Short, kitschy fairground story

Doctors at the funfair
Not a doctor's story, but somehow.

The Goddess of Love at the Fair
A fair with a mystical flair
(this book)

In Love with Costumes
Romantic encounters at a cosplay event

Doctors at the Funfair
Ulrich Germania

Fair of Hearts
Ulrich Germania

www.ingramcontent.com/pod-product-compliance
Lightning Source LLC
Chambersburg PA
CBHW051335160726
47995CB00004B/1089